This
Really
BITES

Publication Date: April 8, 2019

AQUARIOTS
U N L I M I T E D

ISBN-13: 978-1-7750252-8-3

Contents

Chapter 1 – A Walk In The Park. 1

Chapter 2 – When Things Get Hairy. . .13

Chapter 3 – Turning Point. 23

Chapter 4 – Alpha Male. 31

Chapter 5 – The Stroke of Midnight. . .45

Chapter 6 – Wolf Gang. 55

Chapter 1

A Walk In The Park

Today was the day. He was finally going to talk to her.

Tyler Lowell went over the words he'd planned as he followed a sunlit path through the expansive mid-city park, hand clamped on the handle of his lunch cooler. He kept on the lookout, hoping he'd come across the park ranger on one of these paths; he'd seen her in passing several times before on his daily walks.

Finally, Tyler spotted her coming his way. His heart leapt with both nerves and delight. She looked so pretty and professional in her park ranger uniform, with her yellow ballcap and her brown hair in a ponytail.

As she neared, Tyler briefly lifted a hand. "Uh, excuse me...you're the local expert on parks, right?"

She paused with an accommodating look on her face, thumbs in her belt loops.

Open with an indirect compliment— check. "I was just wondering if I'm allowed to picnic here."

She raised her eyebrows a little. "Sure, there's no regulation against it. As long as you don't leave any litter."

"I just figured it's better to ask permission than forgiveness, right?"

She looked faintly amused. "Oh, is that how that saying goes?"

That's right, keep her talking. Make it a conversation. "The only problem is, I brought way too much lunch. Would you care for some of it?"

She paused. Then her mouth rose into a

2

bit of a savvy smile. She glanced at his cooler. "What kind of snacks you got in there?"

She's interested! Tyler kept his tone casual. "Oh, you know, the usual: salad, sandwiches, juice boxes."

"Tempting..." She continued to meet his gaze, voice playful. "But unfortunately, I'm not allowed to fraternize when I'm on duty."

Make another offer! "What if I walk the same way you're going while you continue your patrol, then?"

She pursed her lips, adjusting the bill of her cap. Then she nodded. "That would work."

Yes! As they turned to stroll along together, Tyler switched the cooler to his other hand so he could surreptitiously wipe his clammy palm on his pants.

"Do you always go trolling the park for dates?" the ranger prompted.

Tyler gave a sheepish chuff. "No, I just come here on my lunch hour to get away from the hustle-bustle. And I happened to notice you making your rounds a few times too."

She studied him more closely. "Oh yeah, I think I've seen you around before."

He brightened, straightening. "You remember me? It's only fair that I give you a name to put to a face, then. I'm Tyler."

"Linda."

A classically pretty name. "So, what's it like being a park ranger? Do you meet a lot of bears and cougars?"

She laughed. "I wish! We don't get many of those around here, being in the middle of the city and all. But it's still big enough that it has its own ranger division like the one in Central Park."

"Have you ever had to hunt down a rogue animal?"

"Only with a tranq gun. I don't hunt for sport." A squirrel was hopping along on the grass, and Linda smiled at it. "I love animals. That's why I'd never eat one."

"Oh, I'm a vegetarian, too," Tyler

4

remarked.

She eyed him sidelong. "Really? You're not just saying that to get on my good side?"

"No, really. I've never eaten a scrap of meat in my life. That's why I'm so scrawny, see."

Linda chuckled. "Ah, you're not that bad."

His chest swelled. *She complimented me back!* "Those sandwiches I mentioned are totally meat-free, too. Sure you don't want one?"

She smiled apologetically. "Hey, my job might be a walk in the park, but it's no picnic."

Appreciative mirth rose in him. *Gotta love a girl who can make puns.*

They drifted to a stop where the path forked. "But I'm on this beat every Wednesday," Linda added. "Between...twelve and one."

With a growing grin, Tyler watched Linda as she turned and went down the other path.

Lightheaded with success, Tyler headed

5

out of the park before his lunch break was over, returning to the tech company building across the street. It was his first job out of college. Not the kind of place his ex-roommate Jax would've worked—but despite Jax being the jockish type, they'd become good friends in the dorm. Tyler turned pensive. Jax had mysteriously dropped out just before graduation, and Tyler hadn't heard from him since. From time to time, Tyler still wondered what had happened to him.

When Tyler got back to his desk at the office, he started unpacking the sandwiches to eat while he worked.

His rangy buddy Dwight came by, his lank black hair gleaming in the pale fluorescent lighting. He had a habit of moussing it—as if that would make him look more cool. He folded his arms atop the cubicle partition when he saw Tyler's cooler was still full. "Ah no, did she turn you down?"

Tyler looked up and preened. "On the contrary, I've got a date with her next

Wednesday."

Dwight's face broke into a wide grin. "All right, man!" He gave Tyler a high-five. "Way to use your nerd charm! Maybe there's hope for the rest of us after all."

***

That night, Tyler took a taxi to the park to look at the stars, since the sky was still clear over the city for once. It would be a good spot to bring Linda on a date sometime. He became so mesmerized by imagining it that before he knew it, it was past midnight. On his way back, Tyler kept to the lit paths.

A shape emerged into the light of a nearby lamppost. Dark brown fur bristled thick and ragged, but it wasn't a dog. Its eyes gleamed golden. A wolf.

Tyler froze. What were you supposed to do when you encountered a wild predator? Play dead, or make yourself big? Or did that only work with bears?

The wolf started growling.

Eyes wide, Tyler slowly backed away.

But with a bark, the wolf lunged after him. Tyler whirled and bolted. His heart was pounding as fast as his feet, but he didn't get far before the wolf leapt at his back and bowled him over. Tyler hit the ground, the breath knocked out of him.

He rolled onto his back, lifting one arm to shield his face. Pain shot along his forearm as the snarling wolf sank its teeth into his skin. He cried out in terror. *I'm going to be mauled to death!*

Tyler struggled frantically to kick the wolf off. His knee caught it in the underbelly, and the grip of its jaws let up. He wrenched himself free, curling up into a ball with his arms over his head. At least that way, he could protect his internal organs.

He cringed, tense and waiting in the darkness for the scrape of claws on his back. But a minute passed, and nothing happened. There was only silence.

Cautiously, he shifted his arm and peered out from behind it. The wolf wasn't there. Tyler lifted his head, then rose up on one elbow, looking all around. No sign of it. Relief flooded him.

He scrambled to his feet, wincing at the hot pangs in his forearm, then dashed for the park exit.

Tyler cradled his wounded arm. He couldn't believe that had just happened—or that he'd survived. But he needed to do something about the bite.

As soon as he made it to the road, he waved down a cab and told the driver to take him to the clinic. But if Tyler told them it'd been a wolf, would they believe him? What was a wolf doing in the park, anyway?

He had to report this to the proper authorities before the wolf attacked someone else. His heart jumped. Would Linda be all right?

He hoped she wasn't on duty at night. He only knew her Wednesday beat; even if he went to warn her tomorrow, it could take him hours to find her. And he didn't want to go back into the park alone, lest he encounter the wolf again.

Tyler started shaking. *The shock must be setting in.*

When he got to the clinic, he took a seat in the hall and had to wait for the better part of an hour before he could get in to see the doctor.

The doctor peeled back Tyler's sleeve to examine the bite mark. When Tyler told him what had happened, the doctor glanced up. "A wolf? In the middle of the city?" He sounded skeptical. "Are you sure it wasn't just a dog?"

"Dogs don't have yellow eyes!"

The doctor's brow furrowed, and his mouth drew into a thin line. He probably got all kinds of crackpots spouting claims that were just the product of overactive imaginations or hallucinations. "Well, whatever it was, you should inform Animal Control. If it would bite a human, it could be rabid."

The doctor cleaned and bandaged Tyler's wound, then gave him a rabies shot and sent him on his way with instructions to return three more times over the next two weeks for follow-up shots.

Tyler called Animal Control, and the representative assured him that they'd set up a perimeter around the park and coordinate with the park rangers in the morning.

By the time Tyler got back to his apartment, all he could do was simply flump down on the bed.

Chapter 2

When Things Get Hairy

Tyler shuffled into the dim en-suite bathroom the next morning, still groggy.

Glimpsing himself in the mirror, he did a double take. There was a quarter-inch growth of new stubble on his chin. Tyler leaned closer, lifting a hand to touch it.

"What the...?" He'd shaved just the day before. It couldn't have grown that much overnight. Then he noticed the hair on his head looked shaggier than it had been. Frowning, he sank his fingers into it. He'd have to get a haircut soon.

~ *This Really Bites* ~

After shaving, he carefully slid his shirtsleeve on over his bandage and took the bus to work.

He'd been at his desk for about an hour when he began to feel a prickling sensation along his arm. He absentmindedly scratched at it, but when the itch became too aggravating to ignore, he pushed back the cuff of his sleeve—and stared. His forearm was now streaked with long dark hairs. He'd never been a particularly hairy guy. Were his hormones finally kicking in? He'd never heard of it taking this long. He was twenty-three, for Pete's sake!

When Tyler got back home that evening, he saw that some stubble had already grown back. The worry lurking with him worsened. He shaved for the second time that day—then went straight to his laptop and looked up medical conditions involving excess hair growth. After half an hour, all he found was hypertrichosis, but rabies shots didn't have that side effect, and he wasn't on any other medication.

That, and he came across a link to...lycanthropy. That gave him pause. The impossibly rapid hairiness had only developed after he'd been bitten by a wolf.

Could it be?

Tyler shook his head, scoffing. *Of course not!* What was he thinking? Werewolves only existed in fiction, where they belonged.

The following day, he heard on the news that the park was open again, since the rangers had found no sign of a wolf in it. Tyler was sure there had been a wolf, though; he had the bite mark to prove it. If it really wasn't in the park anymore, where could it be? What if it was now roaming the streets of the city?

"In other news, the search continues for the unknown perpetrator believed to be responsible for several gruesome killings in nearby Slate City—"

Tyler switched off the TV. He didn't need to hear more bad news.

Over the next few days, Tyler got hungry more often, even an hour or two after a meal. He had to eat nearly twice as much to appease his appetite. Was this another symptom related to his hair growth? It was like going through puberty all over again!

One night when he came back from the supermarket, he made it through putting away the groceries before he realized he hadn't turned the lights on. Tyler paused and looked around. He'd been able to find his way easily, without bumping into anything, as if he could actually see the furniture as lighter shapes in the blackness. Frowning, he went over and flicked on the light switch anyway. He must have just been familiar enough with the apartment to navigate it instinctively.

Oddities aside, Tyler was still counting down the days until next Wednesday. He made sure to be on the same path as before, on time, to meet Linda. They walked together and got to talking, and found they had a lot of interests in common: astronomy, board games, and techno music among them.

But Tyler started eyeing the surroundings with some unease. He hadn't been back here since the night the wolf bit him. Was it still around somewhere?

He attempted to sound casual. "I, uh...heard you guys were searching the park for a wolf."

Linda frowned. "There *was* a reported sighting last week, yeah. But we haven't come across anything yet. It's a big park. It could just be a stray dog, or a false account. It better not have just been some chump prank-calling us, and causing all that fuss."

Tyler held a rather guilty silence.

"I don't even know how a wolf would get in here, through the whole city. Still, we're advising people not to go walking in the park at night."

Tyler rubbed his left forearm. *No kidding.* Though it had only been a week, the

17

bite mark had mostly healed up. "So do you think we shouldn't keep meeting each other here?"

Linda looked over at him with a smile. "I wouldn't say that. I'm a ranger, after all; as long as you're with me, I'll protect you."

Tyler quirked his mouth wryly.

"Besides, even if there *was* a wolf, maybe it's moved on by now."

He gained a little reassurance from that. If it still had been here, they would have found some trace of it after a whole week. *Right?*

In the days that followed, Tyler started noticing everyday smells that had been too subtle for him before: someone's wool clothes on the bus, the stale, rain-dampened sidewalk, even the fruity gum under a bench across the street. He had no idea how or why he had developed this enhanced sense, but it didn't go away.

He even overheard gossip in the office, only to find the whispering culprits halfway across the room. He could hear the bus driver chewing a mint, and later someone typing on a keyboard in the neighbouring apartment. It started to drive him a little crazy, despite how he tried to ignore it. The world had already been loud and smelly enough before!

One time, Tyler opened his en-suite door—and it broke off one of its hinges. Dismayed, he tried to prop it against the wall, but he ended up dislocating the doorknob too. *It can't just be shoddy installation.* He lifted his hands off and had to go about everything even more gingerly than he usually did. The other perceptions might have just been his imagination, but this was something physical.

Tyler was so concerned that during his last follow-up visit to the clinic, he took a chance and told the doctor about all his recently developed symptoms. The doctor said he'd never heard of a disease presenting all those signs. There was hormone therapy to hinder hair growth, but that might be more trouble than it was worth. Tyler insisted they do a blood panel to rule out any serious conditions, although the results wouldn't be ready for about a week.

Tyler soon got tired of shaving twice a day and decided to give up on it altogether. By the end of the second day, he had a half-inch scruff covering his chin. But at least, it didn't seem to get longer than that, which was a small consolation.

The third time he met with Linda, she eyed him curiously. "Forgot to shave?"

He scratched at his beard. "Yeah, I guess I'm trying to grow it out."

"Well, it suits you. I like a little scruff on a man, anyway."

Tyler grew a grin. "Really?" Maybe it was good for something after all, if Linda was partial to the rugged outdoorsman look.

Five days later, Tyler got a call from the clinic reporting that his blood test had come back free of any disease markers—and in fact, he seemed to be in perfect health. It was only a slight comfort that there was nothing medically wrong with him. But that still didn't explain his symptoms, and the only other possibility was something he didn't want to think about.

Chapter 3
Turning Point

Tyler awoke to tight cramps in his gut. He sat up with a groan. His skin prickled all over. He clambered out of bed, toppling the clock on his nightstand onto its back. The numbers glowed 12:00. Tyler squeezed a hand on his bare side. This was worse than just indigestion. Was his appendix bursting? He shuffled across the carpet, crossing the square patch of pale moonlight that streamed in through the window. He staggered against the bureau opposite the bed, knocking off a lamp. His whole body was sore, like all his muscles had been put through an intense workout.

He dropped to all fours, panting. It felt like his face was falling off. At the same time, it was as if he was being pulled up by the ears. He squeezed his eyes shut. His legs seemed to be shrinking, and there was the sensation that thick hair was sprouting from every inch of his skin. All his bones ached, as if they were being either stretched or compressed.

Then it was over.

Tyler caught his breath in the sudden reprieve.

Then he lifted his head to look at the standing mirror, and saw a brown wolf staring back at him.

He stayed stock-still, dazed. How had a wolf gotten into his apartment?

Then he realized it was the only reflection there.

When he lifted his arm, the wolf's foreleg lifted.

He *was* the wolf.

~ *Turning Point* ~

Holy crepe! He meant to shout it, but it came out as a lupine yelp as he stumbled back a few steps.

This couldn't be happening. He must be in a dream.

Maybe he could pinch himself to wake up. Not that he'd ever tried to see if that worked before. Then he looked down at his forepaws. How was he supposed to pinch himself when he had no fingers? Tyler lowered his head and nipped at his own foreleg with his canines. But despite the sting, the nightmare didn't end—even when he tried several more times with increasing desperation. He heard whimpering noises and realized they were coming from him.

Tyler turned, and something clattered to the floor; he looked back to see his tail had swept his phone and keys off the footstool at the end of the bed.

He circled again. *This is crazy!* What was he going to do? If any of the stories were to be believed, there was no cure to change back into human form, other than waiting it out.

The light of the moon caught his eye, and he looked up. Mesmerized, he drifted to the window that opened onto the fire escape, and settled onto his haunches.

He drank in the sight of the full moon, and felt an overwhelming urge to howl at it. And, tossing his head back, howl he did. He longed to go outside and run under the moonlight, to feel the wind on his fur. But the balcony only had a ladder, and there was no way he could climb down that in his current state. He doubted he could even turn the apartment doorknob to get out the other way.

Besides, he couldn't risk being seen as a wolf roaming through the building. At best, they'd call Animal Control. At worst...there could be some hunter with a shotgun down the hall who might fancy himself a hero. And Tyler also couldn't let himself loose on the city. He still seemed to be in control of himself, at least

—and he hadn't felt any desire to eat people yet —but if he really was a werewolf, there was no telling what might happen.

Brisk knocking hammered on the door, and Tyler whipped his head around. "What's all the racket in there?" the superintendent's voice called through the wood. "No pets allowed, Lowell!"

Tyler's heart raced. The man had better not use his master key to come in! Tyler ducked under the bed and made sure he was far enough in that his tail was out of sight too. But if the super entered, he'd still see the mess and undoubtedly look around for a dog. Tyler stayed silent and just hoped the man would go away. His wolf ear twitched toward the door when the super's footsteps receded down the hallway again.

Relaxing, Tyler crawled out to pad across the carpet. But he still had nowhere to go.

He started pacing. He was officially

freaking out now. The minutes dragged on and turned into hours, and the panic in him grew. Why wasn't he waking up? His dreams never lasted this long. This couldn't be real. But the creeping dread began to sink in. What if it was? Would it be permanent? He couldn't spend the rest of his life as a wolf! It couldn't have come at a worse time. He was just getting his life together—he had a good job, a decent apartment, and now he was on his way to having a girlfriend. What would Linda think if she knew? No girl in her right mind would date a werewolf! This could ruin everything!

Tyler growled. And so did his stomach. He darted to the kitchenette, but the pads of his paws slipped on the smooth tiles, and he ended up skidding into the cupboards. He collected himself and stepped more carefully to the fridge, claws clicking on the floor. He reached for the fridge handle—only to remember his paw would be useless for opening it. How frustrating it was to not have human hands.

~ *Turning Point* ~

Eventually, he managed to push the magnetic door open from the side with both paws, and poked his snout in. He took the frill of a bread bag in his teeth and pulled it out, then clawed it open to get at the slices inside, which he wolfed down. Tyler brought out a plastic peanut butter jar in his jaws, then sank his fangs into it and ruthlessly ripped out a panel from its side. He stuck his muzzle into the hole and gobbled up everything he could get at. Next he batted out a carton of milk, and it burst open on the floor, sending the white drink pooling out where he could lap it up.

Tyler devoured everything he could get his paws on, until finally he'd eaten his fill. Feeling pleasantly drowsy, he left the fridge open and drifted back into the other room with his head low, then hopped onto the footstool and the bed. He turned around and laid himself out there, then set his muzzle down on his forepaws.

After a brief nap, he opened his eyes,

but to his disappointment, he was still a wolf. There went his last hope that it was something he could wake up from. Then again, he'd had dreams before where he'd woken up, but he'd actually still been dreaming.

A few hours later, dawn lightened the sky out the window. Tyler's skin prickled again, and he sat up. It felt like his body was stretching out, his fur receding into his skin, but it was painless—even refreshing. When it was done, he looked down at himself. To his immense relief, he was human again. He wasn't wearing anything, though. His pants had slipped off when he'd first transformed. That could become inconvenient. Tyler hastened over to the bureau and got out another pair to put on. Then he went back over to the mirror to make sure he really was all back to normal. No more fur, no more wolf ears. But his stubble was just as scruffy as ever. Scratching at it, he gave himself a wry grin. He never thought he'd be so happy to see his lanky physique again.

Chapter 4
Alpha Male

Tyler started awake to his techno ringtone. He lifted his clock. "Oh, geez." It was ten in the morning already! He scrambled out of bed to pick up his phone from the floor. "Yeah?"

"Hey, man, what's keeping you?" Dwight asked. "You'd better get here before the boss notices you're an hour late!"

"I know! I'll be right there!" Tyler threw on his clothes, and a knock sounded on the door just before he yanked it open.

"About all that noise last night," the superintendent began firmly. "I hope you don't

think you can keep a dog here under my nose."
He peered suspiciously past Tyler's shoulder
into the disorderly room.

He thought up a quick explanation.
"Uh...yeah, a stray mutt followed me home, but
he was more trouble than he was worth. Don't
worry, it won't happen again. I dropped him off
at the animal shelter already." Tyler sidled past
the man and hustled off to the elevator.

Tyler stayed up that night, dreading that
the same thing would befall him again. Sitting
on the edge of his bed, he watched as the clock
turned twelve, and braced himself. That's when
it had happened before. But nothing changed.
Once it was getting close to one o'clock, he
began to relax. Maybe he only turned once a
month, when there was a full moon. That was
the traditional myth. Or maybe it had been
nothing but a dream after all. Or some mix of
sleepwalking and a psychotic break, anyway,
since the room *had* been trashed when he
awoke.

~ *Alpha Male* ~

He still saw Linda the next Wednesday. She finally gave Tyler her number, and they started talking on the phone for hours every day after work, until they became quite close.

On Monday, Tyler woke at midnight to the same prickling sensation. He shot upright. *No! It's too soon!* It had only been a week! But there was nothing he could do; he turned into a wolf again—this time without any of the aches, at least. He sought to somehow leave evidence that he was actually a wolf, and it wasn't just in his head, so he could verify it in the daytime. Like taking a photo of himself—but he couldn't work his phone's touchscreen with his paw. Then he thought of leaving an impression of said paw in something like clay, but he didn't have any lying around. He settled for a cheesecake—and indeed, the imprint was still there the next morning. The reality of it finally sank in. This really was his life now.

Then it became every night that Tyler started turning, from midnight to dawn. He tried to make sure he woke up on time, but the lack of sleep meant he often ended up napping on the job later. His work performance lagged. He even enlisted Dwight to wake him whenever necessary.

He still managed to make it out at noon that Wednesday to meet Linda in the park; that was one appointment he wasn't willing to break. When he was with her, he felt like himself again, while they just talked about their lives and thoughts.

At one point, Linda paused under a tree, and Tyler turned back to her. She stood rather near, looking up at him with an admiring eye. "You know, I can't resist shaggy hair," she remarked, and reached up to sink her fingers into his thick locks. The stirring strokes felt refreshingly good on his scalp. Her other hand rose to play with the ends...then she inched her face a bit closer.

Tyler started smiling with anticipation, heartbeat rapidly quickening. *Does that mean what I think it does?* Suppressing his fluttering nerves, he leaned in too, and they shared a tender kiss. The touch of her lips sent a sweet thrill leaping through him, and it wasn't long before his head felt light.

When he met her eyes again, she looked like she'd be amenable to another one.

But then Tyler drew back, remembering himself with a twinge of guilt. He disentangled her fingers and lowered her hands.

"Uh...I'm a bit shy about PDA," he murmured. He couldn't in good conscience let her get involved with him, not when he was a werewolf—and when she didn't know it. He shouldn't have even continued seeing her at all after he'd found out for sure.

Linda watched him with an amused smile. She linked her fingers with his, holding his hand as they resumed strolling. After a moment, Tyler gave her hand a little squeeze too.

Though he'd had no problem staying

awake while with Linda, by midafternoon he was dozing with his head on his desk again—until Dwight shook his shoulder.

Eventually, Tyler decided to try tiring himself out in his wolf form so he would be ready to get to sleep afterward, like walking a dog that had too much energy. He took the subway to the park before midnight, then found some secluded bushes to conceal himself in, where he took off his clothes and tucked them away. After he transformed, he trotted out into the open.

With his wolf eyesight, he spotted a grey rabbit sitting huddled in the grass, motionless but for its twitching nose. A juvenile impulse sent Tyler charging at it. Its long ears perked up, and it launched into a bounding run. He kept after it, head low and four legs pumping. He became exhilarated by the thrill of the chase, the sheer freedom of movement as a wolf.

Then he realized the rabbit probably

didn't consider this just play—it must be terrified of him, thinking him a predator. Tyler slowed to a stop, letting it go on its way. It wasn't like he actually wanted to eat it. He'd never tasted meat in his life, and he had no craving for it now, even in his wolf form. He was grateful for that, because it meant he wouldn't be tempted to prey on humans either. Although, he would've expected the condition itself of being a werewolf would bring with it the uncontrollable desire to eat flesh; that's what most fiction had established to be the case. Then again, he'd never heard a story about a vegetarian being turned into a werewolf, and what that would be like.

Eager to test out his wolf form, Tyler turned and lolloped off through the dark. He ran around in the park for hours, working all his muscles, weaving between trees and leaping over rocks, hopping up and over benches or prowling in the bushes. It was almost fun acting like an animal. He *was* one in body, but he still thought like a person.

He still had to avoid being seen by the occasional homeless person or drunk—the only ones who were wandering the paths this late. But long before he saw them, he could smell their unwashed clothes or cheap booze, and made sure to steer clear of them accordingly.

After getting his fill of exercise, Tyler paced along with his nose low to the ground.

He caught a whiff of a musky scent, and lifted his head, sniffing. Grass rustled, and a pack of seven wolves emerged from a stand of trees ahead. He stared at them, unsure if he should run. Were these regular wolves? Fleeing might just prompt them to chase him. If he stayed, would they consider him one of their own, or would they be able to tell something was different about him?

They came padding over to him in a ragged formation. Then he heard a gruff voice— but not with his ears. It spoke in his head. *There you are, newbitten.* Somehow, Tyler was sure it came from the shaggy brown wolf on the left. *We've been waiting for you to come out and play.*

With a twinge of unease, he took a step back. They were definitely werewolves. And they knew he was one too. What did they want?

We're about to go on the hunt, a tawnier wolf added. *There's plenty of small game to be had here in the park, to keep our skills sharp. Join us!*

But as they got closer to him, their glowing yellow eyes narrowed. They slowly circled him, sizing him up. They were larger than him, and they all looked so strong and intimidating. For the first time, Tyler was aware of how wiry he was in his wolf form.

You smell like prey, their thoughts hissed.

He's a leaf-eater! one greyish wolf put in.

A big auburn wolf fixed his gaze on Tyler. *It's time you embraced your true wolf nature. Become one of us!*

Ears laid back, Tyler whimpered. *No.*

It was a feeble thought, but they heard it anyway.

The others started growling. *No one resists the Alpha!*

They began closing in on him, snarling, and Tyler cringed where he stood. If they attacked him, there was no way he'd get out of it alive, even if he'd known how to defend himself.

Wait!

A dark brown wolf stepped forward. Tyler recognized him—not just as the wolf that had bitten him that first night, but his voice—his *essence*—was that of his former college roommate.

Jax? he wondered, disbelieving. His fur was even the same colour as he remembered Jax's hair had been.

Let me talk to him, Jax went on to the others. *I'm the one who turned him; he's my*

40

responsibility.

The circle grudgingly parted to let the two of them confer aside.

Listen, don't try to be a lone wolf, Jax told him. *You might not like the idea of following orders, but being part of this pack will afford you more security and brotherhood than you've ever known. You won't get a better offer.*

That's not it! I don't want to tear into live animals with my bare teeth. I'm not an animal!

Yes, you are!

No, I'm not! I'm just a guy in wolf's clothing!

Believe me, our way beats the alternative. Most other packs prey on humans. We're one of the good ones.

Tyler stared at Jax. *Why did you do this to me?*

His jaws parted in a wolf grin. *When I recognized you in the park after all these years —and so soon after our pack moved here—I realized it was the perfect opportunity. I wanted us to be friends again, and for you to experience the life of a werewolf too. I know it's the best thing that ever happened to me!*

Tyler's hackles bristled. To think, it hadn't just been some random, unavoidable animal attack, but that his own friend had purposely singled him out for this cursed existence... *You had no right! I didn't ask for this! I never wanted to be a werewolf!*

Well, you are one now. You'll come to realize what an honour it is to be chosen.

I don't want to be part of a gang. Tell them to leave me alone! Tyler turned aside.

Jax was unfazed. *I can buy you a few days to think about it. But then I know you'll make the right decision!*

Tyler took off into the trees, leaving the pack far behind. The sky was beginning to lighten. He had to get back to his clothes before dawn came.

He charged into a clearing, but stopped

short when he spotted a figure off to one side. Linda. She raised her tranq gun. Tyler stared at her, frozen. *Don't shoot, it's me!* he wanted to plead. But as Linda looked into his eyes, she hesitated, squinting. She lowered the gun slightly, and Tyler loped off into the woods again. Once he was out of her sight, he let out a breath. If he'd been tranqed, he would've turned back into his human form with the sunrise, and then his secret would have been out!

Chapter 5

The Stroke of Midnight

After the close call with Linda, Tyler wasn't sure he'd be able to act like everything was normal if he met with her again. She'd seen him in his wolf form. *She* didn't know it had been him, but still.

It was wrong to keep stringing her along. He had to make a decision. Did he dare tell her? What if she had him committed? Should he just break up with her for her own good? But shouldn't he leave that choice up to her? He deliberated for days, and still hadn't come to a conclusion. He couldn't afford to see her until he did.

When he didn't show up next Wednesday, his phone rang. It was Linda. He eyed it guiltily, but didn't answer. She called a few more times over the next couple hours. Then a text popped up on his screen.

Didn't see you today. u ok? Not coming down with something, I hope?

It might be simplest to just drift out of her life. But he didn't want to stay away. And it wouldn't be fair to her to end their association without an explanation. Especially if she liked him as much as it seemed.

After a while, a chirp announced another message from her.

There've been more wolf sightings in the park lately. Is that why you didn't meet me there?

It was agonizing to keep ignoring her, all the more so because he imagined how it must seem to her, and what she must be feeling.

A few minutes later:

46

That's probably better. I even saw one the other day. That's one of the things I wanted to tell you. Call me when you can.

Frustrated dissatisfaction built within him. He'd never had to keep secrets before this happened to him. He cared too much about Linda to go on deceiving her. She was going to find out eventually anyway. Either she would actually stand by him in spite of it—and it would be better that she heard it from him—or she'd understandably opt out of continuing to see him, and it never would have worked in the first place. His condition wasn't going away. It was time to come clean.

That day after work, Tyler headed into the park and tracked her down, following the tangerine scent of her hair conditioner.

When Linda saw him, her expression lightened. But once they neared each other, she said, half-teasing, "Have you been avoiding me?"

"Yeah," he admitted. "I've been avoiding

47

everyone." Tyler stuffed his hands in his pockets. "Listen, there's something I've got to tell you." He took a deep breath, and lifted his eyes to meet hers. "I'm a werewolf."

Linda looked at him very oddly for a long pause. "Is this some kind of roleplaying fantasy of yours or something?"

"No, I mean it," he insisted. "I turn into a wolf every night—fur, paws, tail and all. I can show you, but it only happens after dark. And we should do it somewhere we can be alone."

She turned her head to eye him sidelong. "Are you trying to get me to come back to your place?"

Tyler shook his head, face growing hot. "It's not like that!" He gave a frustrated sigh, desperate to make her understand. "Remember that brown wolf you saw by the trees, Friday morning?"

Linda frowned. "How did you...?"

"That was me. Thanks for not tranqing me, by the way." He offered a small smile. "I'm

48

not a danger to anyone, trust me."

She looked down. "I do trust you, Tyler. I just hope for your sake that you're not as crazy as you sound."

"You'll believe it when you see it. Meet me here in the park just before midnight."

They got together at 11:50 p.m. in a secluded area, but in the light of a lamppost, so she'd be able to see it clearly when he transformed. Linda wore jeans and a form-fitting grey hoodie. She looked even nicer in off-duty clothes.

"Now, once I change, I won't be able to talk, and I won't turn back into a human until sunrise, so...don't freak out and *shoot* me or anything, all right?"

Linda raised her eyebrow. "Lucky for you, I didn't bring my gun," she replied wryly.

"Good. But I'd also prefer it if you didn't go running off to report me to anyone, either," he went on. "Promise you won't?"

"Whatever you say," she agreed

49

dubiously.

Tyler nodded, then proceeded to pull his shirt up over his head.

Linda looked a bit taken aback. "Why are you taking your clothes off?" She eyed his bare chest with some interest, though.

"Sorry, but it's either this, or they get torn."

She shook her head. "You are *so* weird," she scoffed.

Tyler put his toe to his heel to push his shoes off too, but left his pants on.

After standing around for a while, Linda crossed her arms. "Is something supposed to be happening?"

He was looking over his shoulder at the park's post clock. "It will, any minute now." The hands reached twelve, and all his hairs stood on end. Fur bloomed from every pore of his skin, and his body morphed until he stood on four legs as a wolf.

Linda's mouth slowly dropped open,

and she backed away. "No way..." she breathed.

Tyler watched her, worried she'd run screaming from him. He sat on his haunches so Linda knew he wouldn't make any sudden moves. He kept his muzzle down, trying to look as harmless as possible.

Then Linda paused, studying him. "You *are* the wolf I saw before." She took a small step toward him. "No wonder something about those eyes reminded me of you." She ventured the rest of the way up to him, then cautiously extended a hand, lowering it onto his head.

His ears dipped to the sides, and he half-closed his eyes. All the tension left his body at the soothing feel of her smoothing his fur.

"It really is you, isn't it?" Linda murmured.

Tyler tilted his head to nuzzle against her leg. It was a relief to know she wasn't afraid of him.

Once she seemed to have gotten used to him being around her in his wolf form, Tyler took a few steps away and looked over his shoulder at her, waiting until she understood his suggestion and followed. They went for a walk together, with Tyler padding along beside her like a loyal dog. Linda watched him with a smile of wonder, and often rested a hand between his ears. They played around too, running and leaping about and dodging around trees like a fantasy adventurer with her animal companion. Judging by Linda's grin, she found it as fun as he did.

Eventually, they settled down on the grass, and Linda talked to him for hours, looking into his golden eyes and stroking his fur. But later, she ended up reclining on her back and falling asleep with one arm tucked under her head. Tyler stayed up to keep watch. After a while, he gently laid his muzzle on her midriff, which rose and fell slightly with her soft breaths. Affection welled in his heart. He was so lucky—not only that she was dating him at all, but that she didn't even mind that he was a werewolf. Who else but a park ranger would think that was cool?

Once the stars began to fade, Tyler nudged Linda's face with his nose. She stirred, and lifted her head abruptly, then smiled in fond recollection, setting a hand on his head. "I still can't believe my boyfriend is a wolf."

They revisited the place he'd left his clothes, and Linda turned her back so he could put them on once he became human again.

Tyler cleared his throat. "Okay, I'm decent."

Linda turned back to him, and beamed. "It's good to have you back," she said softly, and wrapped her arms around him.

He held her too, marveling that showing her his wolfish side had actually brought them closer together.

Chapter 6
Wolf Gang

Tyler was preparing supper in his kitchenette, while the small TV on the counter related the news in the background.

Upon hearing something about the park, he looked at the screen to see it showing a tarp-covered body. He snatched the remote and turned up the volume.

"...the site of a grisly murder," the newswoman went on. "The victim appears to be a homeless man who lived in the park. As of yet, he is otherwise unidentified, due to the extent of mutilation to what remains of the body.

Officials believe it was an animal attack—but the question remains, what kind of animal in the city could have done such damage?"

Tyler got a sinking feeling. The only thing it could have been was...a wolf. He grabbed his phone and called Linda. The tightness in his chest relaxed when her voice answered. "Linda here."

"Hey, I just heard about the body on the news. Are you all right?"

"Yeah, I wasn't there when it was discovered. But we're going to continue investigating along with the police."

Tyler suppressed his worry. "Just don't go into the park after midnight, okay?"

"Why? Do you know something?"

He balked, gaze drifting down, so filled with hesitation it was like he was holding his breath. The longer his indecision lasted, the more the tension made him disinclined to speak.

"It didn't have anything to do with you,

did it?" There was an abrupt edge to her voice.

Tyler lifted his head. "Of course not! I'm still in control." But he couldn't keep it from her now. He tried to think of a way he could phrase it over the phone. "But...there are others like me. A pack of them lives in the city."

"What?! Why didn't you tell me?"

"But they wouldn't do this!" Tyler went on. "They only hunt animals."

There was a pause. "How sure are you of that?"

Not sure enough.

Over the next week, there was a new murder every night, some even in alleyways in the city. It definitely wasn't an accident. Tyler decided to do some investigating of his own. He used his phonebook app to look up Jax's number, and anxiously drummed his fingers on the dining table as he waited for the line to connect.

"Y-ello?"

"Hey, Jax. It's me."

"Tyler?" Jax sounded surprised, but delighted. "It's good to hear from you, buddy! Have you made your decision?"

Tyler furrowed his brow. "No, that's not what this is about. Have you heard what's been happening in the park?"

"That wasn't us, man." His tone was sober. "It must be another pack. You know, the kind I was telling you about? We've caught a few glimpses of them encroaching on our territory. The boss doesn't like it, but we've been steering clear of them. They're probably the ones from Slate City."

Cold dread gripped Tyler's stomach. It was even worse than he'd feared. "They came here?" he breathed. "Do you know who they are?"

"Nope. Wouldn't know 'em if I saw 'em —in *daylight*, if you know what I mean. Would if I smelled them, though," Jax added thoughtfully.

"Is there any way we can stop them?"

"Nothing to do but go up against them. But I doubt they'd get scared off. They'd make it a fight to the death." Jax was silent for a moment. "There's more of them than there are of us. We could really use you on our team, bud."

Tyler sighed in aggravation. "You know I can't."

"They're killers, Ty! They won't have a problem offing us too!"

Turmoil filled Tyler, urgency warring with resistance. He couldn't abandon all of them to be murdered by the others—but he couldn't make himself a fighter either. "There must be some other way," he insisted. "Do they have any weaknesses?"

"You mean like silver bullets? Nah. That's a bunch of hooey. Regular bullets would still do the trick, though."

Tyler tried to think of an alternative. If they could somehow find out the werewolves' human identities...maybe they could tie them to the crimes that way, and convict them as people. There was only one place they could be sure to find them. "Tell the pack to meet me in the park this Thursday. After midnight."

The next day, Tyler met with Linda, and together they worked out the rest of the plan. It would mean revealing the existence of werewolves to the authorities, but it was the only way.

On Thursday night, she drove him to the park in her ranger van. On the way, he transformed into a wolf in the passenger seat. Linda brought her tranq gun as they headed into the park together, but she stayed back in the trees while Tyler cautiously continued forward to meet the waiting pack.

One of the wolves started growling. *I smell a human.*

And tranq darts! another added.

Why did you bring her here? the auburn-furred Alpha demanded of Tyler. *Do you mean to betray us?*

~ *Wolf Gang* ~

Some of the wolves lunged toward Linda, but Tyler darted out to block them. *No! She's here to help!* When they paused, Tyler looked each of them in the eye. *Listen, this new pack is a threat to us all. You want them gone, right? But you can't defeat them on your own. I have a plan. I'll help you get rid of them, on one condition. You'll let me stay a lone wolf.*

The Alpha stared at him for a long minute, golden eyes glittering. *And what might this plan of yours be?*

While you tackle them, Linda will tranq them so they can be put in a cage. She'll wait until your pack is long gone before calling in reinforcements. Then we can make sure they never terrorize this city again.

Alpha eyed the copse Linda was in. *It better work,* he said grudgingly. *If it does—and only if it does—then we have a deal. Honour among wolves.*

Tyler's heart leapt with success.

The wolves stiffened as the wind

brought a scent of raw meat. They turned to face the new pack that emerged on the far side of the clearing. There were nine of them, and they were all larger and brawnier, with dark brown fur that was noticeably redder.

Linda slowly came up beside Tyler, tranq rifle held at the ready.

The werewolves started toward the intruders, and the two packs drifted to a stop a few yards apart.

This is our territory, man-eaters, the Alpha growled. *Leave the city, or we'll make you leave.*

The other pack leader curled his lip in a sneer. *You think you runts scare us?* He turned his eyes to Tyler. *And what is this I smell? A leaf-eater? You're a disgrace to the wolf form. And your only other backup is a human girl with a toy gun? You're the ones who won't leave here alive.*

The man-eaters charged, and Alpha's pack leapt to meet them. They collided in a

62

vicious flurry of snarls and teeth and fur and claws. The smell of blood and fear soon filled the air, stinging Tyler's nose. Several ganged up on the man-eater alpha to bear him down and leave the others without direction. Linda took aim, and as soon as they had him subdued, Tyler told the wolves of Alpha's pack to back off, so Linda had a clear shot at the right target. They did the same whenever Alpha's pack had one of the man-eaters pinned.

The opponent wrestling with Jax bit deep into his neck, then threw him off. Jax hit the ground with a whimper, and Tyler's gut lurched. Then the man-eater charged at Linda while she was reloading.

No! Tyler raced toward them, fear gripping his heart.

The man-eater leaped at Linda, toppling her onto her back and sending the rifle flying out of reach.

Oh God, if it bit her, she'd turn into a werewolf too...

~ *This Really Bites* ~

Tyler collided with the werewolf, knocking it off Linda, and they landed in a tumble. Snarling, the wolf surged up and sank its teeth into Tyler's foreleg. He let out a pained yip and tried to claw at the wolf with his other paw, but the wolf didn't let go. It was going to tear him to shreds!

Then the wolf went limp, slumping to the ground. Tyler looked around to see Linda propped on one elbow, tranq gun pointed their way. Tyler's ears sagged with relief and gratitude. She must have been able to tell them apart, even in the dark.

Tyler limped over to rejoin her side as she got to her feet. She targeted the other man-eaters, and they resumed their strategy until every last one was sedated.

Alpha's pack licked at their wounds. Tyler checked on his own leg, but it was already beginning to heal, even faster than the original bite on his arm had.

At Tyler's request, Alpha's pack went to

sniff out where the man-eaters had left their clothes. When they brought back the nine pairs of pants in their jaws, Linda searched the pockets for wallets. They had driver's licenses in them, so they now knew who all of the men were.

While the others dispersed, Linda used her radio to call in the other park rangers so they could help her load the wolves into the large iron cage in the back of the van. Tyler lingered; he didn't want to leave her alone with the man-eaters.

Linda looked at him, and smiled. "Go on, Tyler. I'll be fine. These tranqs are strong enough to keep an elephant knocked out for hours." She patted her rifle, which was still pointed at the wolves. "And I still have some left over, just in case."

Tyler met her eyes for another moment, then turned and loped off into the trees. But just before he reached the horizon, he looked over his shoulder. He stayed hidden in the thicket and watched until the reinforcements came before he withdrew to a far corner of the park.

***

Tyler met with Linda the next evening, outside the ranger station near the park. "How'd it go?" he asked, rather anxious. "Is the investigation underway?"

Linda's mouth twisted wryly. "Not quite. Representatives from some government agency I've never heard of showed up and confiscated them. Apparently, we're not the only ones who know about werewolves."

Tyler stared at her, filled with even more unease.

"Don't worry, I didn't tell them about you," Linda went on. "Or even the other pack. They're long gone by now."

Tyler softened, touched that she'd done that for him. But a trace of uncertainty gnawed at him. "Are you sure you still want to date a werewolf?"

Linda stepped closer and looped her arms atop his shoulders with a contented sigh. "Why wouldn't I? You're the nicest werewolf I've ever met." She leaned in and gave him a kiss.

Tyler looked at her with a growing smile, his hands resting on her waist. "So, how would you like to go have a great big salad at The New Leaf?"

"I'd *love* to," Linda declared. They turned to stroll away together, each with an arm around the other. "I hear they have great turnovers."

The End

ABOUT THE AUTHOR

Maddie Benedict is a Millennial who has been writing fiction ever since she was little. She loves animals, and, unsurprisingly, she's a vegetarian, which she has been her whole life. She's never met a werewolf, but if she did, she'd only like the harmless kind.

This is the second of several short stories she's written to date. She has hundreds more ideas where that came from (and also where other ones came from), which she expects will keep her busy for the next century or so.